Once upon a time, a writer felt scared. But standing by the writer's side was a friend who gave the writer courage. The friend's name was Sarah Lanier (who later became Sarah Goodrich). Dear friend, thank you. Write the novel. With love—K. W.

For Sonia Chaghatzbanian
—J. C.

Margaret K. McElderry Books
An imprint of Simon & Schuster Children's Publishing Division
1230 Avenue of the Americas
New York, New York 10020

The text for this book is set in Adobe Caslon.
The illustrations for this book are rendered in acrylic paint.

Manufactured in China
0615 SCP
10 9

Library of Congress Cataloging-in-Publication Data
Wilson, Karma.
Bear feels scared / Karma Wilson ; illustrated by Jane Chapman.—1st ed.
p. cm.
Summary: Bear's animal friends come to his rescue when he becomes lost
and frightened in the woods.
ISBN-13: 978-0-689-85986-1
ISBN-10: 0-689-85986-4
[1. Fear—Fiction. 2. Lost children—Fiction. 3. Friendship—Fiction.
4. Bears—Fiction. 5. Animals—Fiction. 6. Stories in rhyme.]
I. Chapman, Jane, 1970– ill. II. Title.
PZ8.3.W6976Bb 2008
[E]—dc22
2007028951

Bear Feels Scared

Karma Wilson

illustrations by Jane Chapman

MARGARET K. MCELDERRY BOOKS

New York   London   Toronto   Sydney

*I*n the deep, dark woods
by the Strawberry Vale,
a big bear lumbers
down a small, crooked trail.

Bear's tummy growls
as he looks for a snack.
But it's cold, cold, cold,
so the bear turns back.

He is not home yet when the sun starts to set. . . .

And the bear feels scared. . . .

Bear shakes and he shivers
as a storm starts to howl.
Bear mutters, "What is that?
Are there spooks on the prowl?"

The path gets dimmer
and the sky grows gray.
Bear looks to and fro,
but he can't find his way.

He huddles by a tree and he wails,
"Poor me!"

And the bear feels scared. . . .

Meanwhile, back
in the warm, cozy lair,
friends start to worry
for their poor, lost Bear.

"It is late," Mouse squeaks,
"and our Bear doesn't roam."
"There's a storm!" cries Hare.
"Shouldn't Bear be home?"

Wren tweets from his perch, "We must all go search!

What if Bear feels scared?"

The friends bundle up
and begin to prepare.
They form a search party
for their lost friend Bear.

But Bear is all alone
and he sheds big tears.
There's a noise in the forest
and he feels big fears.

Bear trembles in the wind. How he longs for a friend.

And the bear feels scared. . . .

Badger lights a lamp
and he shouts, "Let's go!
All the birds search high
while the rest search low."

With a flounce and a flutter
they set off together.
They trudge down the trail
through the wild, wet weather.

They call, "Ho, Bear, are you there? Are you there?"

And the bear feels scared.

But he perks up his ears.
Is it Mole calling out?
And is that Hare's voice?
Does Bear hear him shout?

Wren, Owl, and Raven
all squawk from the sky:
"It is Bear! He is there!"
And they sigh big sighs.

By a tree waits Bear, ten feet from his lair!

And the bear
looks
scared.

With a flap and flurry
all the friends gather near.
They give him bear hugs—
they calm his bear fears.

Later in the night,
all clustered in a heap,
the bear spins stories
while his friends fall asleep.

Cuddled up tight, they snore through the night.

And the bear
feels
safe.